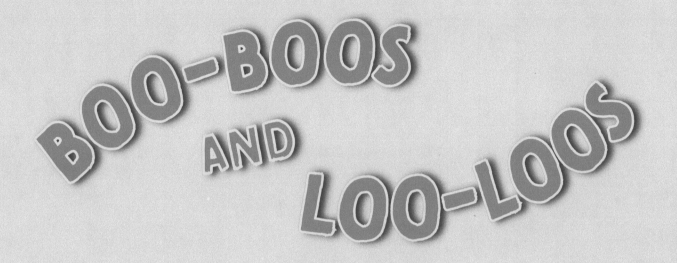

BOO-BOOS AND LOO-LOOS

Written by
Cindy Lou

Illustrated by Pranisha Shrestha

Boo-Boos happen now and then
A Band-Aid or a hug helps them mend.

A Whoops comes with no pain or distress
It's just a slip of the hand and a little mess.

Oh, but a loo-loo that's
another thing
A loo-loo has its own song to sing
A loo-loo needs time and attention
you know!
A loo-loo takes planning and
scheming to grow.

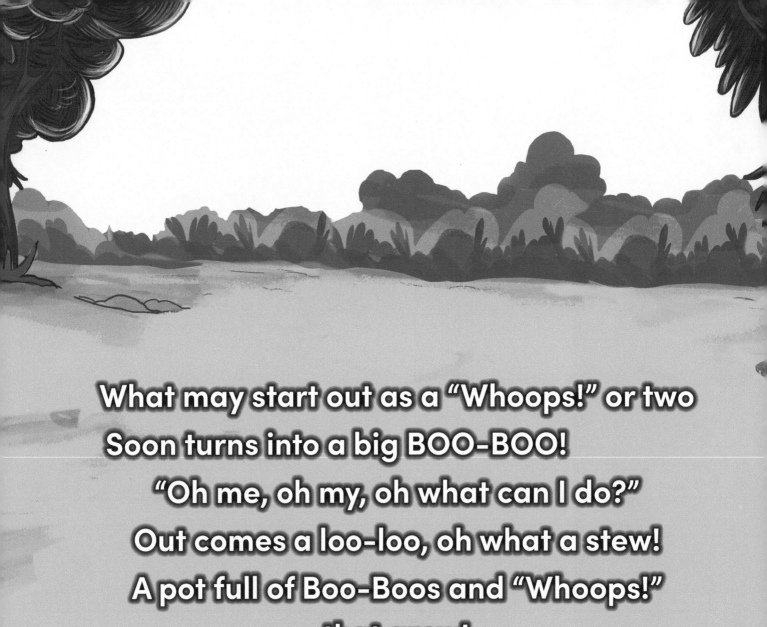

What may start out as a "Whoops!" or two
Soon turns into a big BOO-BOO!
"Oh me, oh my, oh what can I do?"
Out comes a loo-loo, oh what a stew!
A pot full of Boo-Boos and "Whoops!"
that grew!
A problem, called a Loo- loo!

When a loo-loo appears before
your eyes,
Thoughts of defeat, feel bigger
than your size!
You want to cover your head and
wear a disguise,
With the hope the loo-loo will find
its' own demise!

But make no mistake, a second look
you will take
You will see the loo-loo is still here!
It may have just moved a little
over there!
It takes trust and some wisdom
from the past
To realize that this won't last

You can learn from all of this
really fast!
You may slip or fall from your
choices of thought
You will discover what works well
and what does not!

Boo- Boos, whoops and loo- loos
are just that!
Thoughts that become a matter
of fact!
A thought with a feeling, a great
plan indeed!
A plan and a thought that travels
with speed.

Across the sky, in the dark of the night
The yet to know becomes your flight.

Through ups
and downs and
twist and turns
Oh My!!
There is so
much to learn!
Choices and
decisions to make
So many
adventures
to take!

Then with a whisper
from inside
You step off the fearful ride,
With a grin on your face
You realize creating a loo-loo
is no disgrace!

Learning from those moments of dismay
Is how we find our way!

Loo-loos and boo boos are two
different things
But when you throw in a "Whoops!"
you may just create your dream!

 FriesenPress

One Printers Way
Altona, MB R0G 0B0
Canada

www.friesenpress.com

ISBN
978-1-03-915277-9 (Hardcover)
978-1-03-915276-2 (Paperback)
978-1-03-915278-6 (eBook)

1. JUVENILE FICTION, STORIES IN VERSE

Distributed to the trade by The Ingram Book Company

Live your best life!

CPSIA information can be obtained
at www.ICGtesting.com
Printed in the USA
BVHW012317090123
655957BV00001B/15